Topic: Life Skills　　　　　**Subtopic:** Healthy Habits

Notes to Parents and Teachers:

As a child becomes more familiar reading books, it is important for him/her to rely on and use reading strategies more independently to help figure out words they do not know.

REMEMBER: PRAISE IS A GREAT MOTIVATOR!

Here are some praise points for beginning readers:

- I saw you get your mouth ready to say the first letter of that word.
- I like the way you used the picture to help you figure out that word.
- I noticed that you saw some sight words you knew how to read!

Book Ends for the Reader!

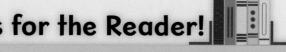

Here are some reminders before reading the text:

- Point to each word you read to make it match what you say.
- Use the picture for help.
- Look at and say the first letter sound of the word.
- Look for sight words that you know how to read in the story.
- Think about the story to see what word might make sense.

Words to Know Before You Read

baby

brother

change

habits

helper

practicing

rules

sister

Katie Can
KATIE IS A BIG SISTER

By Erin Savory

Illustrated by
Marcin Piwowarski

ROurke
Educational Media

A Division of
Carson Dellosa
Education

Katie has big news.

"My mom is having a baby!" Katie says.

Grandma picks her up from school.

6

"Time to meet your baby brother."

8

Katie is excited.

Life will change with a
baby at home.

But Katie can
learn new things!

Katie has Down syndrome.
Practicing new habits
helps her learn.

12

She is ready to learn to help with the baby.

"Meet Kevin."

"Hi, Kevin. My name is Katie.
I am your sister!"

15

There are new rules
in Katie's house.

WASH YOUR HANDS

OWN-UP HAS
HELP YOU HOLD
KEVIN
3. No LOUD SOUNDS
DURING NAP TIM

Wash your hands before touching Kevin.

A grown-up has to help you hold Kevin.

No loud sounds
during nap time.

Katie follows the rules.
She is a great helper.

Katie is the
best sister!

# Book Ends for the Reader

I know...

1. Who picks up Katie from school?

2. What is Katie's little brother's name?

3. What is one of the new rules in Katie's house?

I think...

1. What is a big change that you have experienced?

2. What helps you learn new things?

3. What is one way you can help out at home?

Book Ends for the Reader

What happened in this book?

Look at each picture and talk about what happened in the story.

About the Author

Erin Savory is a writer who lives in Florida. She knows all about being a sister, because she has three brothers and three sisters, including a younger sister with Down syndrome. Erin's siblings are her very best friends!

About the Illustrator

Marcin Piwowarski is an illustrator from Poland. He finds inspiration in nature and music. Marcin has worked on numerous books, including *Who is Ana Dalt?*, *You Belong*, *The Mouse in the Hammock*, and *Dibs*. He hopes his work will allow children and adults alike to explore fascinating and familiar worlds.

Library of Congress PCN Data

Katie is a Big Sister / Erin Savory
(Katie Can)
ISBN 978-1-73164-899-0 (hard cover)(alk. paper)
ISBN 978-1-73164-847-1 (soft cover)
ISBN 978-1-73164-951-5 (E-book)
ISBN 978-1-73165-003-0 (e-Pub)
Library of Congress Control Number: 2021935279

Rourke Educational Media
Printed in the United States of America
01-1872111937

© 2022 Rourke Educational Media

www.rourkeeducationalmedia.com

Edited by: Hailey Scragg
Layout by: Janeen Ruggiero
Cover and interior illustrations by: Marcin Piwowarski